Dear Parent:

Here is a book which addresses a pertinent subject for many families–a new baby in the home.

One of the good things about reading books together as a family is that the book can be the focus of a discussion. Experts say that reading a book such as *Arthur's Baby* can be an opportunity to talk about shared experiences: what was it like when I was born? Did Grandma come to our house when you were in the hospital? Or, what will it be like when the baby comes home? Will I be able to help?

This book isn't purely informational, however. More than anything, *Arthur's Baby* is a good story. Readers will meet Arthur (the aardvark) and his irrepressible sister, D. W. We feel sure your children will enjoy this book by Marc Brown, one of the country's most popular creators of children's stories.

Sincerely,

*Fritz J. Luecke*

Fritz J. Luecke
Editorial Director
Weekly Reader Books

Weekly Reader Children's Book Club Presents

# ARTHUR'S BABY

## MARC BROWN

Little, Brown and Company

Boston   Toronto   London

## ◇FOR TOLON, TUCKER AND ELIZA◇
### my three babies

This book is a presentation of Newfield Publications, Inc.
Newfield Publications offers book clubs for children from
preschool through high school. For further information
write to: **Newfield Publications, Inc.,** 4343 Equity Drive,
Columbus, Ohio 43228.

Published by arrangement with Little, Brown and Company (Inc.).
Newfield Publications is a federally registered trademark of
Newfield Publications, Inc. Weekly Reader is a federally registered
trademark of Weekly Reader Corporation.

Library of Congress Cataloging-in-Publication Data

Brown, Marc Tolon.
    Arthur's baby.

Summary: Arthur isn't sure he is happy about the new baby in the
family but when his sister asks for his help in handling the baby,
Arthur feels much better.
    [1. Babies–Fiction.  2. Brothers and sisters–Fiction] I. Title
PZ7.B81618Aok 1987        [E]        87-3988
HC: ISBN 0-316-11123-6
PB: ISBN 0-316-11007-8

*Joy Street Books are published*
*by Little, Brown and Company (Inc.)*

HC: 10 9 8 7 6 5 4
PB: 10 9 8 7 6 5 4 3 2

WOR
*Published simultaneously in Canada*
*by Little, Brown & Company (Canada) Limited*

Printed in the United States of America

"We have a surprise for you," said Mother
and Father.
"Is it a bicycle?" asked Arthur.

"We're going to have a baby!" said Mother.

"Ooooo," squealed D.W. "I love babies!"

"A *baby*?" said Arthur.

"Yes, in about six months," said Father.

"Plenty of time for us all to get ready."

Arthur's friends had lots of advice.
"Better get some earplugs," said Binky Barnes,
"or you'll never sleep."

"Forget about playing after school," said Buster.
"You'll have to babysit."

"You'll have to change all those dirty diapers!"
said Muffy.

"And you'll probably start talking baby talk,"
said Francine. "Doo doo ga ga boo boo."

For the next few months, everywhere
Arthur looked there were babies — more
and more babies.
"I think babies are taking over the world!"
said Arthur.

WAA WAA WAAAAAA!

"Don't look now," said Buster,
"but you could be in for triple trouble."

One day after school, D.W. grabbed
Arthur's arm.
"I will teach you how to diaper a baby," she said.
"Don't worry about diapers," said Mother.
"Come sit next to me. I want to show you
something."

Arthur age 9 months

"Is that really me?" asked Arthur.
"Yes," said Mother. "You were such a cute baby."

Arthur age 1 year

D.W. age 2 months

"Look," said D.W. "This is me with Mommy and Daddy. Don't I look adorable?"

D.W. age 5months

That Saturday morning, Mother took out her suitcase.

"Where are you going?" asked Arthur.

"The baby could come any day now," said Mother. "I need to be ready for the hospital."

"Here," said D.W. "Something for you to look at while you're there."

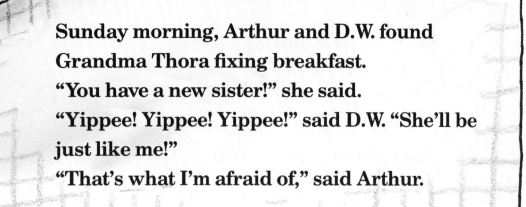

Sunday morning, Arthur and D.W. found
Grandma Thora fixing breakfast.
"You have a new sister!" she said.
"Yippee! Yippee! Yippee!" said D.W. "She'll be
just like me!"
"That's what I'm afraid of," said Arthur.

The next day, they went to the hospital to see the new baby.

"We named her Kate," said Father.

"I think she has your nose, Arthur."

"I think she has D.W.'s mouth," said Arthur.

On Tuesday, Mother and Father brought Kate home.
Everyone was acting like they'd never seen
a baby before.
Every time the doorbell rang, more presents arrived.
"They're not for you, Arthur," said D.W.
"They're for the baby."

"Arthur, don't you want to try holding Kate?"
Mother asked.
"Can I have another turn first?" asked D.W.
"It's Arthur's turn," Mother said.
"I'd rather look," said Arthur.
"It's just as well," said D.W.
"Arthur doesn't know beans
about babies."

A few days later, Mother needed some help.
"I have to go upstairs," she said. "Arthur, would
you watch Kate?"
"*Me?*" asked Arthur. "What do I do?"
"Don't worry," said D.W. "I'll take care
of everything."

When the doorbell rang, D.W. answered the door.
"Arthur can't play," she said. "He has to babysit.
But you can come in and see my baby."

"Don't get too close, because you all have germs!
And be quiet," D.W. said, "my baby is sleeping."

"Look!" said Francine. "She opened her eyes."
"Stand back," said D.W. "She wants her bottle."

Kate drank her bottle in a flash.

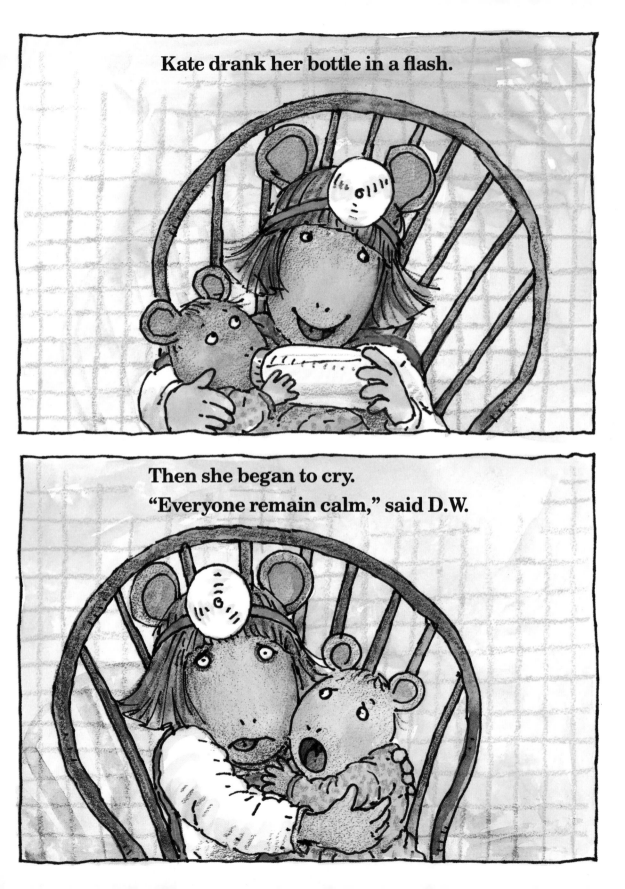

Then she began to cry.
"Everyone remain calm," said D.W.

D.W. gave Kate a kiss.
Kate cried louder.

D.W. bounced Kate.
Kate screamed.

"Arthur, quick! Do something!" D.W. said.
"She's your baby, too."
"All of a sudden she's *my* baby," said Arthur.
"Why is she crying?" asked D.W.
"She's trying to tell you something," said Arthur.
"What?" asked D.W.
"Listen carefully," said Arthur.